EVACUATION

EVACUATION

BORIS CHRONICLES™ BOOK ONE

PAUL C. MIDDLETON

MICHAEL ANDERLE

DISRUPTIVE IMAGINATION

LMBPN Publishing
PMB 196, 2540 South Maryland Pkwy
Las Vegas, NV 89109

First US edition, March 2016
Version 3.03, March 2021
Print ISBN: 978-1-64202-959-8

CHAPTER ONE

TQB Base Colorado - USA

Michael had been right. Hitting these cowards from the rear was fun. More fun than Boris had enjoyed in years.

The merc at 'tail-end Charlie' sensed something coming up behind the group and turned to fire at whatever was stalking them.

In his momentary shock at seeing what looked like a standing bear, Boris grasped the barrel of his rifle in one of his pawed hands and wrenched. Pulling the mercenary toward him, Boris impaled the man with his free hand, slung the rapidly-dying man off to the side, and dropped the gun.

It was killing time.

Death on two legs advanced with determination. Boris planned to kill the mercenaries attacking the base as they came within his range. His muscular legs propelling him forward, the mercs found that it was difficult to hit him without shooting a teammate. The tight grouping forced on them by the tunnel became another foe. They were finding out how deceptive the speed of a bear could be, while Boris's movement was even quicker than that of an ordinary animal. Most humans who saw Boris in his brutal glory had seconds of shock before they had to react or die.

The confusion he was causing must be helping the defenders ahead. Boris was glad to be helping Michael, glad that the *svolic* he had been working for would get their comeuppance.

Send him to kill children, would they? Especially children under Michael's protection or this woman who had finally captured his attention. If he had time, he'd offer his services to help hunt them down.

His roar of joy reverberated down the narrow confines of the hallways. The pain of his constant headache was overcome with the chemical cocktail that saturated his body in this shape. The fear of those in front of him was a scent that exhilarated his ferocity and crammed him with a wicked cocktail of both rage and relief.

Then, suddenly, his ability to constrain his actions while in this form was lost when a bullet fired from someone in front glanced off his skull and the headache he had been suffering overcame everything.

In his pain, he lost it. Lost control, lost his mind, lost his humanity and ability to think.

The headache flared, and he roared in maddened anger, charging forward through the squad. Sending bodies, arms, heads, and legs flying to bounce against the walls, the blood of the dead splashed high to coat the rock walls with a picture of life passing.

He reached the one that had shot him and ripped his attacker's head from his body.

Standing on his back feet, he roared in anger at the decapitated head and crushed the skull with his paws in revenge.

There was a cresting wave of pain as he felt himself shifting back to human form. Slowly, he dropped to the ground and fell into unconsciousness surrounded by a bed of bloody body parts.

Eric and a handful of the new Queen's Guardians were doing a sweep of the corridors to confirm that all the attackers had been killed, and none were hiding.

He and the small team of Guardians turned a corner to see a scene of destruction and death. Walls splashed in blood, bodies torn in half. Flesh, blood, and parts were everywhere.

Eric was impressed. This hallway might qualify as being as bloody a mess as Bethany Anne had left in Costa Rica that time she went berserk.

Eric could hear one Guardian at the back throwing up. Their noses had told them what to expect, but the visual impact was something else. Some stomachs and people would never be the same. Never enough mind bleach to clean up this kind of memory.

Eric noticed one whole body in this jumble. It was a large man, bearded and partially nude. He had blood seeping from his eyes and dripping from his ears, clothes torn, but no significant wounds. The lead Guardian paused at the body and knelt down to touch the neck, "This one's alive boss... and he's a bear!" He turned to look at Eric, a question on his face.

Eric stepped over and looked closer, "Shit. That's Boris. He helped Michael get the kids back and warned us about the nuke." He felt relief that the mercenary had survived. At least Boris was not a casualty as well.

Eric paused for a moment to consider before reaching up to his shoulder and clicking on his radio, "Lance, it's Eric. Do you think you and TOM can ask Bethany Anne if we can put Boris in the medical pod? It looks like Michael's support is severely injured, and I'm for giving him whatever it takes to help him all things considered."

Lance responded immediately. "ADAM is already spoofing the satellites, and Bethany Anne agrees. It might be nice to salvage something positive out of all this shit."

Back on the Polaris, Bethany Anne had told TOM to shut her feelings down. She was still hurting, deeply, but could not take the time she needed to feel those emotions now.

Later. Later, she would take the time.

They still had to sort out a lot of things on the base and ships. She turned to Stephen and asked, "So what do you know about Boris?"

Stephen paused and then shrugged "I haven't heard much recently about him. Honestly, I hadn't considered much about the Russian situation with all of the other issues we have been fighting. I was there when Boris challenged Michael. So was Peter, one of our original brethren." His vision clouded briefly in grief.

Stephen continued his commentary as he bit down on his hurt, "He was trying to prove himself to his Pack leader more than anything. I consider him an honorable leader for his people. He leads them and continues to protect those sworn to him. Peter, our late brother, mentioned that he preferred having Boris deal with Nosferatu problems and the younger Forsaken. With Boris, it's all professional and very little emotion. Some of Peter's other people would try to do a rush job to impress, and fail to get the little details accomplished."

Stephen sighed, "He is also the only Pricolici I know of who managed to master the change for more than a century without succumbing to the temptation and madness. I warned him of the danger, and he apparently listened. When I last asked Peter, he admitted 'that's why I still need to use others. Four years in five I can call on him'. I suspect that is why he took mercenary work. Staying in his human form may be an asset to controlling the mixed shape for him."

He shrugged "When he gets out of the pod we should ask him."

"What about the people, the town, he protects. Do you know what that is all about?" Bethany Anne asked.

Stephen said, "Yes, but it would be better if you can wait and let him tell his own story on that." Bethany Anne nodded her acceptance.

"I'm going to go pick him up," she told Stephen, starting to walk toward her suite, "Please ask the captain to announce over the speakers that Ashur needs to meet me there."

Moscow, Slums

Janna was sitting at a desk, going over the most recent

collection of data she had grabbed from her subordinates' drop points. A mailbox here, a capsule buried with a USB drive inside it under a specific tree in the park there, things like that.

As an officer in the GRU, the military intelligence division of the Russian army, she didn't want to be where she was right now. If she hadn't crossed paths with her uncle four years ago, she wouldn't be, dammit. Somehow, he'd recognized her as his missing niece. Abandoned by her parents when she was eight, Janna had survived on the streets, mostly surviving on the kindness of the librarians in the library she took refuge in during the day. They'd slipped her food, and in winter given her shelter in their own homes on occasion.

Over the years she'd read nearly every book in the library. Some of them she hadn't understood. But they gave her an enormous knowledge base. She was still happiest reading a book in a warm bed.

When she'd turned fifteen, it had been getting steadily harder for her to turn down the advances of some of the pimps on the street, who wanted to add her to their stable of whores. Instead, she went to a recruitment office for the regular Army and managed to convince the recruitment officer she was seventeen despite a lack of papers. She'd specifically picked her outfit to make it look like she was off a farm, and it wasn't that unusual, even today, for someone from a farm to not have a birth certificate or any official documentation at her age.

Her test scores had been solid, although she had deliberately blown some of the questions. Too much knowledge would have blown her cover as coming from the farm and being taught by her parents, even though she claimed one of her grandparents was a former professor.

She'd been accepted and been put into the stream for a version of Spetznatz training given to some women. Life on the streets had given her a wiry, but muscular, frame for a woman. Being on the streets had been a constant struggle, and the fear of ending up back there had pushed her to excel throughout basic training.

She'd ended up graduating near the top of the battalion.

Then, shortly after completing basic training, her path had crossed with her uncle whom she hadn't recognized. He was now a colonel and had identified her by the distinctive birthmark on her lower neck, one she now assiduously covered with make-up.

She'd been brought in, but not as she had expected by MPs. After all, she'd been breaking the law by enlisting at such a young age. More so by lying on her enlistment.

Instead, it had been Intelligence that had been brought in. They'd made all sorts of threats, starting with locking her up. Prison had been the worst thing to use as a threat. Her genuine lack of concern unnerved them.

In her mind, at least she would have three squares and a bed while in prison. It was even possible that she should be able to make contacts that would allow her to find a position in organized crime when she was released. Her marksmanship and unarmed combat scores throughout basic training had been in the top percentile of both sexes. It wasn't that she embraced the concept of joining organized crime, but if that were the only door open to her, she'd take it.

Then they'd appealed to her, somewhat shaky, sense of

nationalism and finally, they'd threatened her uncle's rank and position. In exchange for no action against him or her, she agreed to transfer to intelligence and go through officer training. Very grudgingly. She would far prefer to have remained a grunt, even now.

When she had joined, all she had cared about was three meals and a bed that military life offered her. As well as a path away from the constant harassment of men who thought they could control her. Every thug on the streets believed that.

Now she truly cared for her subordinates. At least all those whom she'd picked herself. Sergeant Brogonovich and the five other men who'd been assigned to her for this mission she didn't trust one bit. She had no idea why those six men had been foisted on her, but for an operation as sensitive as this none of them had the right mentality. They were more likely to join the NVG than investigate it in her opinion.

She still couldn't understand how they'd even made the jump to intelligence. Or at least to her section of it. They were thugs, through and through. She felt a shudder of distaste. She didn't approve philosophically of some of the tactics used by the Russian military to get information. Beyond anything else, they were unreliable and only relevant in time-critical situations. If there was a bomb driving to a countdown, then it could be justified. But torturing people for information with no time-critical results? There was no real point to it. There were better interrogation techniques that got much more reliable information.

The biggest problem she had with Brogonovich and his half squad was that they were Chechen *Chernozpi*, black asses. She was never sure where their loyalties lay, especially with how cagey they were about their religion. For all she knew, they sympathized with the damned Islamists.

Janna shook herself, rose and stretched. Her mind was starting to wander down well-traveled paths. It was time for her to go home and get some rest. The tension that built up in her as she picked up information from the blind drop points always made her feel tired.

Best to get back to the analyses when she was fresh. At least she would have the satisfaction of a job well done.

TOM's Ship, Earth Orbit

Two hours later in TOM's spaceship, Bethany Anne regarded the Russian through the glass. She had walked the Etheric from the Polaris to the base, grabbed Boris, and she and Ashur traveled to the ship. She prepped Boris and stuck him in the medical pod, while TOM explained the settings to use.

TOM spoke up, **The pod has analyzed the nanites in his blood and found them to be similar to the type found in all Wechselbalg. However, their programming differs significantly from that base, altered beyond the necessary for the different form he can take. I can understand no clear reason for that.**

Bethany Anne paced in the room, as TOM continued.

These nanites are more similar in programming to what I had on my ship and injected into Michael. There are two significant differences. The first is that his Etheric draw is stronger than others we have tested. This would probably cause a female so modified to be

more fertile rather than less. Most Weres we have encountered are less fertile than normal humans. The second difference is a form of coercion control that is paused, but still present. The Pod will modify and destroy that programming. His genetic makeup is remarkably close to the original genotype these nanites were designed to support. I posit that this may account for his extended age. It may be that he was born with the nanites in his mother's system, which would have meant less potential for damage and less need for extensive modifications than a post-birth change.

How long until he comes out of the Pod, TOM?

About ten more minutes. Boris had a significant Etheric balance before he went in that has aided the healing process. However, the pod has still not identified what may have caused the initial damage. After he has come out, may I route the information to ADAM to receive his opinion?

Sure, but how about we ask him? Maybe it has happened before. He would be capable of healing from this damage, right?

Yes, Bethany Anne. His existing Etheric charge helped significantly reduce the time required.

Boris woke up. There was a bubble of metal trapping him. He took a couple of deep breaths to calm down and remember what had been happening. He had been taking on a group of mercenaries. Playing with them. Then the pain in his head had grown terribly, and he had lost it.

For the first time in a century or more, he had succumbed to blind rage and couldn't remember anything but bits and pieces of, well, bits and pieces. He cursed at himself in Russian before realizing he was doing it without pain. Pain that had been a constant companion for so long.

He relaxed in the Pod and closed his eyes, reveling in the painless quiet bliss he hadn't known for at least a year.

The cylinder popped open. Boris winced as the headache came back. He blinked several times as his eyes fought to focus against bright light. When they focused, he saw a woman he did not know. She was a great beauty. He thought she must be the one that Michael referred to, this Bethany Anne. Her poise and grace were that of one worthy to be a Czarina.

Boris looked down and realized he was naked, and blushed. "Do you have clothes I can vear?" He asked as he covered himself with his hands. Bethany Anne smiled and pointed to a bench next to the wall. It was a small, but lovely smile, shadowed by pain and loss.

As he got dressed, Bethany Anne asked "Why did you come to America? And on such a risky enterprise. Surely you knew Michael was awake, and if he found your involvement, he might have killed you."

Boris zipped the pants up and put on a belt while thinking of his answer. Finally, he shrugged "It was better than losing my control at home and killing my people, da? Someone would have come after me, and these damned headaches have been getting worse. When I saw the news, it occurred to me this new technology might be the cause. I needed more information on these happenings! I figured there were three options, and one of them left me alive, so I went vith that plan. I fail to see stupidity in that."

"Besides, I have helped. You put me in that cell, da? Why you let me out if you tink I a danger to you?"

Bethany Anne was exasperated. "I know your English is better than that Boris. Knock it off. I've spoken with Stephen and with Michael's death, I have little patience for games right now."

Boris froze, and then two great tears formed in his eyes. He bowed his head, "I am sorry, Czarina. Michael could be a harsh man, could be a dangerous man, but he was a great man. In the short time since I was re-acquainted with him, I saw the joy his love, whom I must assume is you, had brought him." He said in a polished, nearly accent-less English. Bethany Anne nodded and pursed her lips.

"But," he massaged his temples, "These headaches are wearing on me. I can only assume that they are related to the new technology you have created?"

Bethany Anne looked at him, assessing his honesty. At last, she said, "Perhaps we should go and tell the tale to everyone."

"Ashur," she spoke aloud, and Boris raised his eyebrows at the size of the white German Shepherd that walked into the room. "We will get a small team together, Boris. Let me take you back to the Polaris and pull in a few people. We need to stay away from Colorado right now."

Ashur came up to Bethany Anne, who grabbed him with one hand and put a hand on Boris's shoulder and then took a small step into the Polaris. Boris collapsed onto her dressing room floor, grabbing his head in pain.

Fucking shit! Bethany Anne yelled, ***What the hell, TOM?***

With a groan of pain, Boris took his hands away from his ears, his right hand filled with blood.

TOM, does this give you an idea of what happened? He seems to react badly to my stepping through the Etheric.

I can posit a theory. He is sensitive to the Etheric in a different way than Barnabas. I will need ADAM to run through his vital statistics from the medical pod to confirm.

If he is, is there a way you can stop his headaches? He had to be a gottverdam idiot or desperate to run the risk he did for information. He doesn't seem stupid, so I'll go with desperate.

I will see what ADAM and I can determine. I have too little data to be assured we can cure his headaches without permanent damage. I will get back to you.

It took Bethany Anne and Ashur fifteen minutes to grab those she wanted. John, Frank, Nathan, Ecaterina, Barnabas, and Gabrielle joined them in the conference room as Boris was still muzzily shaking his head, trying to release the lingering pain. Ashur dropped to the floor behind her chair, next to the wall.

The others took seats watching Boris.

Stephen opened the conversation. "Boris, what were you doing in the US? We'd all like to know. The real reason, not the mercenary contract. I am satisfied that you didn't know the target. If you had, you would have tried to contact Michael yourself."

Boris nodded somberly, "That is the problem with secrets, sometimes allies unintentionally act against you. I came to the US to investigate the technology that was sending things into space. I had a theory, it might be related to the constant headaches that are slowly driving me insane." He paused and looked at Bethany Anne. "I have a new theory. Might it be that you stepped closer to Siberia several months ago? In early May?"

Bethany Anne pursed her lips, "Yes, I did."

TOM spoke from a speaker in the room, "While you may have exacerbated the problem, Bethany Anne, I doubt that you have been the sole source. Kamiko Kana undoubtedly caused etheric ripples. Boris may be sensitive enough that the Etheric draw of the engines affects him, according to the data from the medical pod."

Sending privately to Bethany Anne, TOM added, **There is a way to fix the problem. However, it will leave him still able to sense changes in the Etheric. The other pathways may change his brain unpredictably. Removing memories or shifting personality. Further, he has the potential to draw on the Etheric while in human form, possibly to the same extent as Gabrielle.**

Of course, we should... oh. Hmm, I guess we don't know enough about him, do we?

Bethany Anne said, "TOM, get with ADAM and see if you can cure the headaches."

Frank asked, "I'm curious. Stephen mentioned a town in Siberia where you protect the residents?"

Boris nodded "Da. I am a Pack leader in Siberia. You must understand, with the wide spaces and size of Russia there is no Pack Council, just packs. And it is worth a non-alpha's life to move across territories without permission."

"But the town and its people?" Boris stared while focusing on nothing, tears appearing in his eyes. "I protect them because of an oath I swore to my love before the *predatel'skaya negodyay* Reds had her executed. I swore I would save as many White Russians from the State as possible. I did, with the help of some Cossacks, I also aid and defend. Most of those I shield are their descendants."

Boris stopped staring into nothing and brought his attention back to those around the table, "The rest are pack. I protect them to honor her memory. 'Tis all I have left." He was silent and contemplative, while Stephen swept the room with his eyes and gave a sharp nod, confirming the story.

Boris continued, "I worked as a mercenary after the war to build up the infrastructure. Also, to send the brightest away for a better education than would be possible in central Russia. Many outside Siberia viewed our town with suspicion. Inside Siberia, everyone descends from *prestup-niki,* criminals of one sort or another, so no-one judges another."

He laid two large hands on the table in front of every-one, "I am bound to them by blood oath and heart oath. I cannot in good conscience swear such an oath to you. I would, to honor Michael and the changes you started in him, swear an oath to aid you in any way I can that is not prevented by my previous promise." He clasped his fist to his breast. Then he said, "Do you have a knife, Czarina?"

Bethany Anne blinked and then turned to Stephen with a raised eyebrow in question, choosing not to read Boris' mind at this juncture as it felt wrong.

Stephen smiled. "He wants to swear his oath the way his mother taught him." Bethany Anne turned towards the door, "John?"

John stepped into the room and unclasped his Bowie,

handing it to Bethany Anne hilt first. As she turned Boris started to stand before going to his knees, eyes shut in pain.

"What the hell?" she asked.

ADAM? TOM?

>>**The Ad Aeternitatem just sent up four Pods for an outer defense.**<<

"Fucking shit." Bethany Anne spoke, "Four Pods just lifted from the Ad Aeternitatem. I'll have them stop that unless an emergency calls for it."

>>**Understood.**<<

"Gott Verdamnt!"

TOM, please tell me we can fix that?

Tom replied while Boris recovered, **ADAM and I have found a solution to the source of the headaches. It will require around two hours in the medical pod.**

Bethany Anne walked around the table holding the Bowie, "Well Boris, I guess after one more trip, we should have a solution for your headaches."

Boris shook his head to clear it and stood up beside her. He held out his hand, palm up and indicated she was to slice his hand with the knife, which she did quickly and with no fanfare.

Boris held a grimace from his face. The Bowie was silver-laced. His English was good, but his Russian accent was very pronounced during his oath, "By my blood on your blade, in memory of Michael, I swear service as I am able to you."

Bethany Anne sliced her own palm, "In honor, I keep your vows as mine. In memory of loves lost, I will protect your people as my own."

Boris froze for a moment and looked at Stephen, his incredulous eyes seeking confirmation.

"Yes, Boris. She means it," was Stephen's simple response.

He took one knee before Bethany Anne, "On this world, my service is yours."

"Oh knock it off, you big bear." Bethany Anne said, with a weak grin as she nodded to John and tossed him the knife. "Let's get you back into the Pod so TOM can fix you." She reached out a hand as Ashur stepped up beside her, "Mind the first step, it hurts like a bitch."

The three disappeared.

CHAPTER TWO

Were training room, QBS Ad Aeternitatem

It took three hours for Bethany Anne to bring Boris back. It had taken another thirty minutes before she realized that Nathan and Peter had plans if Boris was up to sparring.

Bethany Anne wanted to roll her eyes at the testosterone bullshit and then remembered they were, literally, programmed that way. Shaking her head with resignation and a hint of amusement, she left them to their exercises. She needed a status update from her father.

Nathan and Peter were both itching for a matchup. He was an ancient Pricolici. With that age, a mythos had developed around him. Many considered him a rumor or legend, like Michael to vampires in Asia.

How could either one pass up the chance to spar with a rumor? Boris had been around Weres a long time. The feeling of wellness and release from pain energized him. He was agreeable to the sparring session. The prospect amused him. These two were so young. He had centuries of experience over them in all his forms. The only question was how long it would take to defeat them.

They talked and decided Peter should go first, after agreeing to spar as humans for the first rounds. Peter fought well. Within minutes it was apparent Boris was skilled in the styles Peter knew. His counters were muscle memory, and after about two minutes Peter was on the ground for a three-count.

The disappointment was evident in Peter's stance. He had not landed a solid blow. Boris spoke to him after the match. "You are good, youngling. I have learned many styles from different cultures over the centuries. Siberia was the ends of the earth for centuries. People looking to escape the past or start fresh ended up there. I tried for many decades to learn from as many as possible. I guess that I have at least four centuries on you. Do not take it so hard."

Boris then indicated to Nathan that he was ready. This opponent showed more skill and training than Peter, so Boris took time to test his defenses. He found them good. After two minutes of sparring back and forth, he found a rhythm to Nathan's attacks. A weakness in his personal style that Boris could exploit. He let Nathan get comfortable and suddenly switched gears, which threw Nathan enough for Boris to get him in a full nelson. After trying several methods to break the hold and failing, Nathan muttered, "I yield."

Boris released him from the grapple and grinned, "You have spent much time training, but you let yourself fall into a rhythm. It is a weakness you need to be careful of. An experienced opponent will find it and exploit it."

Nathan snorted "And how likely is it I'll find someone as experienced as you?"

Boris shrugged "Not the point. If someone notices it, it is a weakness. I suggest you work on it."

Nathan turned and saw Gabrielle in the doorway, grinning. Nathan looked at her and said "Okay then, you have a go without the tricks BA taught you. Think of it as redeeming our honor."

Boris shrugged and nodded as Gabrielle stepped forward.

They circled each other, watching how their opponent moved. Gabrielle darted forward under his reach and caught an elbow in her chest for her trouble. She backed off again, and Boris feinted with a kick to the midriff that was actually a step forward. He grabbed the arm that reached to grab his foot. Gabriel broke the hold and kneed him in the gut. He folded forward in pain but used the movement to achieve a grapple around her waist. Once her feet were off the ground, held above his shoulders, Boris asked, "Do you yield or should I throw you?" She took a half minute trying to find the leverage to remove his grip without going to vamp speed, but couldn't and called the bout.

She glared at him. "Okay. Rematch. This time, I will use some tricks" She flashed a vicious grin at him. Boris shrugged and nodded. It wasn't like he expected to beat her if she went all out.

Gabrielle picked up the speed to the first level. To her surprise, he could still follow her, and despite her landing more blows, he coped well. He could face Gabrielle despite the step up in speed. He waited, often taking a pounding until she pushed too hard on an attack and left him an opening he could exploit. He punished every blow that used too much force, pulled her too far into a strike, ruthlessly.

Then she realized he was riding most of the blows, robbing them of striking power. After ten minutes of this, they heard Bethany Anne from the doorway.

"I'd call it a draw at that level, Gabrielle. I need to talk to Boris," Bethany Anne commented as the two turned in her direction.

They backed off and bowed. Boris raised a questioning eyebrow, but Bethany Anne shook her head and indicated he should follow her. Walking down the hall, Bethany Anne said "Stephen tells me you have been a Pricolici for four centuries. He also told me of the dangers of the form."

Boris nodded, "I have noticed that you have three amongst you with that form. They have been warned of the dangers?"

"Yes, Stephen cautioned them," Bethany Anne replied, "I am hoping you could provide the new Pricolici insight on how you have managed the complications for so long? They're good friends, and I'm not willing to lose them to madness."

Boris nodded, "I will teach both methods I know. If I could meet them privately?"

Bethany Anne could almost feel his level of discomfort talking about this subject around non-Weres. She smiled and responded, "Of course." Her curiosity was acting up. Her presence for the discussion was unnecessary, and

Boris wanted privacy. If the curiosity became too much, she could always ask Ecaterina later.

The four Pricolici met in a conference room on the Ad Aeternitatem later that evening.

Boris started with the most straightforward means. "One year in five. Stay out of the Pricolici form just one year in five, and you won't lose yourself to it. For most of the first two centuries after I met Stephen this was the method I used."

Staring, Peter asked, "But you found a different method?"

Boris turned and nodded to him "Da. But I'm not so sure it is one available to most. Perhaps it just differs for others. I have tried and failed to teach it at least twice. But, for me, I found a way of changing form without rage. With calmness, like a summer pond without a breeze in the air. When you reach a particular state, you will be able to reach for the form. But I cannot guarantee you will find the same path. It is something each of you will need to discover alone. If you find rage once changed, the benefit is lost. Until you are sure, stay as human or wolf for one year in three. If you do not, you will eventually succumb to eternal rage."

Nathan considered Boris's statements, "You sound more akin to a Japanese Zen teacher."

Boris grinned broadly. "Perhaps, Grasshopper, because it was a half-Japanese woman who suggested the solution to me."

Peter and Ecaterina burst out laughing as Nathan glared at Boris.

Boris continued, "I will think of other circumstances where I have changed and suggested more options if I think they may work. But it is no easy thing. This form is equal measure curse and blessing. Always remember that before you change. Think 'Do I need to? Can I be as effective as a man or a wolf?' The less you use it, the safer you'll be. And if you find yourself behaving more aggressively than average humans, DON'T change. You are near the madness then."

The next morning Boris was having breakfast in the ship's mess with Nathan, talking about moving unobserved. "I think in a city, you are less likely to be noticed than me, Nathan. A man of my size finds it hard to move unobserved. A bear is more likely seen than a wolf and taken as a bigger threat. In a forest, I think I could best you at being unobserved, more because of the time I've had to master it than anything."

"Sure, sure. But you have more mass to hide. Surely we'd be even there?" Nathan replied.

Boris shrugged, "It is not so big a problem if you learn how to deal with it. An interesting assessment of ability, seeing who your pups find first. Perhaps…"

Both men turned when they heard the quick footsteps coming down the hallway and watched the doorway as Frank entered, looked around to find them and hurried over to their table. He nodded to Nathan but turned to Boris, "Sorry to interrupt you guys. Boris, your town is Romanovka, right? The one in Chelyabinsk Oblast?" Boris nodded, his expression tightening in concern. Frank's face clouded up, "Dammit. I've received information the Russian government is rounding up *treasonous dissidents* there."

The entire mess went silent as Boris stood up from the table and loudly spun invectives from five languages. He took a couple of minutes to calm down. With eyes filled with anger, he turned towards Frank. "Do you know who ordered this?" He held up his hand to stop Frank from answering, "It was straight from the President wasn't it?" Frank nodded his head. "I keep telling people that all communists who had served in the bureaucracies should have been shot or imprisoned. Instead, they elect one - and a former KGB at that - to the Presidency!" Boris looked around as if he wanted to spit on something. He found no acceptable options on the ship.

He paused, then walked towards the door. Nathan called out, "Boris, wait! I'm sure Bethany Anne will want to help you!"

Boris turned and shook his head at Nathan, "The politics are complicated. If non-Russians attempted to interfere, perceptions would change. It would result in greater danger to my people. I must go alone. I can make arrangements for a flight. Vassily will regret telling anyone I was dead, the shitehawk arsehole licker."

That cursing, Frank could understand.

Nathan tried again, "We can at least get you there a lot faster than any plane. Let us do that much - and give you a clean line of communications in case we can help you further."

Boris was torn between going there his way and acknowledging the obligation Bethany Anne may feel.

Accepting help was something he was unused to doing. He eventually nodded, following Nathan and Frank as they quickly left the mess and headed towards the hanger.

Frank and Nathan stood while Bethany Anne eyed them both. Her eyes went from one man to the other, her voice calm, clipped, precise. Too precise.

Like a woman trying mightily to hold back anger.

"So, Boris is back in Russia. The government is rounding up his people and killing them, and you two did what, exactly? Supported his effort by getting him to the location as quickly as possible?"

Frank thought he might have preferred to have a discussion with an outwardly angry Bethany Anne, not this calm, cool, and composed woman in front of him. "Well, while I'm good, he is the best we have on the politics in the region. We tossed it to TOM, and he said you were asleep."

TOM, you are back on the couch!

>>**Analysis of situation confirms Boris's belief that outside intervention would escalate the situation. 92.3% probability, margin of error +/- 5.3% due to large number of unknown attitudes of personnel below the rank of Lieutenant Colonel in the region**<<

I gave him my word, ADAM.

>>**Analysis of past known actions by Boris indicate that he is not averse to calling in aid if required.** <<

She continued to stare at both Frank and Nathan for several moments. "Well he'd better contact us within the week, or I'm sending you two to find him and sort the problem out, with or without his blessing. If the situation seems bad enough, I'll make a personal appearance and if the Russian fucking government wants to play hardball? I'll drop heavy rocks on their hard-ass heads."

The men nodded and stepped out of the room. Neither would change the decision they had made, but there wasn't a reason to stick around to rehash the options with her, either.

CHAPTER THREE

Moscow, Slums

Janna cursed herself as she heard a foot scrape on the sidewalk behind her. She hadn't been paying enough attention, and her office for reviewing materials and sending them to the colonel was not in one of the better areas of town. She was glad she habitually kept her hands in pockets and didn't wear gloves.

It seemed she had picked up a small group of thugs. Either they wanted to capture her for their boss or their own stable of whores, or they were merely planning on raping her. In this district, the police would pay no attention to such a crime. They were swamped with a gang war and the murders it produced.

Focused and making sure her Walther PPK-L .32 caliber was ready to be drawn from her sleeve. She was glad it was winter as it allowed her to wear a heavy coat with no comment. It enabled her to carry the light pistol in a holster on her wrist, concealed by the coat sleeve and quickly drawn.

She waited until she could hear them move up close behind her. Without warning, she dropped low and swept her right leg in an arc behind her, knocking two of the thugs into each other. Rolling to her right, she dodged the grab from the criminal on her far left. She drew her pistol as she rolled and steadied herself by leaving her left knee on the ground when she finished the movement. Firing three quick shots from the quiet gun into the brute that had grabbed at her, she took him out of the equation.

"She killed Yuri!" a fourth thug shouted as he barrelled into her. Janna hadn't heard him until a moment before he struck. She avoided his grasping arms, but his body still hit her hard. He knocked her over, sending her tumbling across the ground. The force of his tackle sent the pistol skittering along the pavement.

One of the other thugs growled, "She must be some kinda cop. We'll have to kill 'er now. Siminov will be pissed. He'll prefer the loss over us bringing a cop for 'is stable."

She continued to roll away from the thugs and considered running. A quick glance at them told her running was not a good option. They looked fit for street criminals, and she doubted she could outrun them. The pistol had skittered a significant distance from all of them, teetering on a drain. She quickly scanned the quiet street. She used this route as one of several back to her apartment to avoid attracting police attention. Unfortunately, that had backfired by drawing criminal attention. There was nothing available nearby for her to use as a weapon with her pistol gone.

Then the fourth thug drew what looked to be an American Bowie knife. Problem solved, all she had to do was take that from him. As long as she made sure the blade disappeared or was wiped clean of her prints, the police would write it off as gang violence. Her cover would be completely intact. She discarded her heavy coat. Better to have greater freedom of movement and risk a cold or frostbite than end up dead.

There were two problems. First, Janna needed to keep them separated from her pistol. Second, get out of this alive.

The first problem solved itself in a surprising manner. One of the first two thugs went to the gun, but the fourth assailant ground out, "No! For killing Yuri like that, this lady just became a message. We cut her up good."

Janna snorted internally. The only close combat trainers she'd ever had who'd considered her skills 'barely acceptable' had been from the Spetsnaz. It was one reason she had been chosen to lead the mission.

The two unarmed thugs took on a wrestler's stance. Having trained in Pankration, Janna took a stand somewhere between the traditional Eastern martial artist's side-on stance and a wrestler's stance. If any of these gangsters had done military service, her posture was a dead giveaway to the training. Knifeman's eyes narrowed as if he recognized the stance.

Rather than risk a shouted warning to the other two, she darted towards him. She deflected his reactionary strike with her forearm. The tip of the knife tore through her cheap jumper and shirt, scraping a shallow bloody gash along the forearm. With the uninjured side, she grasped his wrist. Quickly hitting the inside of his elbow with the injured arm, she redirected his knife into his chest.

His expression went from anger, to shock and quickly faded to slackness. The knife sticking out of his ribs must have cleaved one of the great veins or the heart itself for him to die so soon. The sudden, lethal action on Janna's part left the remaining two opponents momentarily stunned. Twisting the knife slightly, she pulled it clear of the dead man's chest.

The two remaining criminals were muscle and dumb muscle at that. They froze with shock at the sudden mayhem that had appeared in their midst.

She rose and faced them, bloody knife in hand. One turned towards the pistol, and the other fled. Taking advantage of the turned back, Janna charged forward jumped on it wrapping her free arm over one shoulder and under the other. She got the knifepoint to his throat as he fell forward with her weight on his back.

Momentum and the combined force of both of them hitting the ground did the rest. She wouldn't be able to recover the knife and needed to be careful to clean it of prints, but he wasn't going anywhere. The tip of the blade was sticking out the back of his neck.

Wiping her bloody hands in the cold snow, she scrambled towards the pistol. She couldn't afford to let the last thug escape. If word reached his boss, she would become a target.

Reaching it, she went to a knee and used her injured hand to steady the shots. It took the rest of the magazine to kill him. She cleaned her hands as well as possible on the dead men's clothes and in the snow. Then she checked her forearm. Luckily it was barely seeping, despite the pain, it was now giving her. She would just have to risk blood getting on the inside of her coat.

Her habit of wearing black clothing would pay off tonight. It was unlikely that people would notice more than moisture in this weather on dark cloth. And with the snow on the ground, damp clothing was unremarkable.

Having done her best to remove evidence of her presence in the fight, she headed home. It would probably be hours before someone else stumbled across a scene given the lack of foot traffic in the area, but she hurried on towards her flat, anyway. Writing the incident report for her superiors would be a pain in the arse. Getting caught up in a police investigation was something she planned on avoiding.

CHAPTER FOUR

Romanovka, Chelyabinsk Oblast, Siberia, Russia

Boris walked into town after being dropped on the outskirts by the black flying thing. He had no idea of how it worked, but it had gotten him back home faster than anything else could have. He needed information. Without knowing what was happening, he was operating in the dark. Without information, any action he took was as likely to endanger his friends as help them.

He walked out to Paul's farm. Paul had been his companion for fifteen years while he had worked as Peter's enforcer. As he walked up, he noticed that none of the lights were on. He sniffed the air and quietly observed the surroundings. Paul was either one of those taken or he had taken his family to his hide.

Boris continued to look around, noticing things that indicated trouble. He kept walking, and when the front door came into view, he made a sour face. The door was smashed off its hinges and into pieces.

Someone had kicked in the door, hard.

He took five minutes to survey the area around the house. The clutter he found didn't tell him anything. Neither Paul nor Alecta had been the best of housekeepers. Their sons were more interested in hunting and riding on horseback than cleaning.

Fortunately, there was no blood. If Paul or his boys had been home when the police had arrived there would have been Blood, Boris was confident. He could only hope all four of them were in the safe site, a lined cellar out in the forest.

Boris would learn what was happening from one of them, either his old friend and partner or Paul's sons. He started the long hike to the east, following no path. He knew his lands, and they talked to him of danger, pain, and retribution.

"… and so they just took her. Why did you go this time? Where were you when I needed you, Boris? They took my wife with no fear of retribution. You know they wouldn't have done that if you were here!" Paul shouted at Boris. At least his headaches were gone now.

Paul had been in the Australian special forces before meeting Alecta. He was also too brave or too stupid to understand the full impact of fear. Boris wasn't sure which. Paul knew Boris was a Werebear and just shrugged it off.

Boris replied as soothingly as possible, "It is as well I did Paul. We now have someone who may help us. At least once we decide to leave or stay. Where are they keeping the people they arrested?"

"In the old militia base on the edge of town. At least a company of soldiers from the West. Those in charge couldn't have trusted local troops." Paul looked up with a weary smile. "Those closest to us have many family members enlisted with the locals, other soldiers local to us are too afraid."

"Memories are long here. Our neighbors know about the lost battalions, ghosts of people taken in the night, secret treaties, and other dark secrets. Far-born troops would not." Boris sighed and looked around. "I will gather the pack. You gather at least one from each family that has had a member taken. We will free our comrades and punish these interlopers. Tell everyone to prepare for a Meeting of Decision. It is time to decide if Russia is where we now belong."

Boris had gathered all of the pack that was local. Siberia was full of wide open spaces, so they numbered about fifty, a far higher number than could be possible elsewhere.

He looked out over the group, their anger radiating from their eyes, their hurt from their hearts. "I come to you, not as your Alpha, demanding your obedience, but as your leader. Asking for volunteers. I will free those the government has taken hostage tonight. The path has risks, but I will not have those under my protection falsely accused, nor leave them to be abused."

"Alpha, they have tanks," Oleg cried out.

Boris snarled, "And we have thermite! I will infiltrate first to remove any threat the tanks pose. If you are willing to attack the soldiers - with support from the families of those taken." He looked at them one more time, his eyes flashing yellow, "Talk amongst the pack."

He stepped off the small box and walked away.

When he returned a half hour later, his second, Danislav, stepped forward. "Boris, we are with you. The scum, these communistic fools," he spat, "will be slaughtered for invading our lands."

As Boris reviewed the final preparations to move and attack the reinforced company of soldiers, a runner from town reached them. He went to Paul and tried to steel himself from the dread grasping his heart at the sight of the panting messenger.

The runner gasped, "More came, Hetman. This afternoon after you left, a platoon marched through town and picked twenty-five people at random. They dragged them to the central square and shot them as foreign agents. No trial. The town has been placed under martial law. The soldier's commander has imposed a curfew but left it to the police to enforce."

Those standing nearest Boris took a step back. The fury on his face was frightening. Those who knew him best felt a brief twang of pity at his expression. He shouted to the gathered force. "We wait only for those who lost blood kin. When we march, my orders are blood and retribution! We will make them pay in blood for our losses, many times over this night. We will teach them fear, the knowledge of what happens when anyone attacks our people! Take the

Captains and above ALIVE if possible. We need to understand if they have gone rogue or are acting on orders from
above. As for curfew, we know the police in our town.
They will not enforce it."

Within the hour Boris' mixed group of Weres and
townspeople started their march toward the old militia
base. All looked forward to bloody vengeance against the
murderers. Rage shadowed the entire force, bending it to a
single goal. Boris and the pack led the way, with over five
hundred townspeople self-organized and following.

Some of the men who had served with him on mercenary operations had pulled out their support equipment.
Whoever these soldiers were, some mortars dropping in
on their barracks would likely ruin their night for damned
sure. Orders were given to avoid targeting the prison
block. Enough people had seen the prisoners being taken
and confined. Some had shadowed the soldiers who took
their kin. Word had quickly spread about where they were
imprisoned.

Boris knew he had to sneak past the sentries and
destroy the communications building and the APCs. If he
could block any call for reinforcements and silence the
heavy weapons, then the screams of those who preyed on
his people would fill the night.

It was a symphony he would hear, or die trying.

CHAPTER FIVE

Militia Base, Outskirts of Romanovka, Siberia, Russia

Boris looked over the camp. The soldiers were acting relaxed. Calm chatter in groups outside the barracks had been seen before the sun had gone down. Perhaps they were too comfortable. They had sentries, but no roving patrols were visible. The assumption must have been the twenty-five executions, and a martial law declaration had cowed the population.

In their arrogance, they had forgotten the power of rage.

This part of Russia was different, and the commanders of these troops did not appreciate the differences. Apparently, they didn't understand his group nor that those in this region of Siberia felt no compelling loyalty to the government. Boris' people were raised to revere the Czars, despite having no worthy heir to swear fealty before.

They trained in the discipline of the best Cossacks. Took in Cossack legends, traditions, and pride with their mother's milk.

Boris nodded and sent his best group of woodsmen and hunters around to the other side of the base under Paul and divided into three troops. The rest of his force had self-organized into four companies, further divided into several platoons each. Plans had been laid to prevent any enemy soldier fleeing. Platoons in each company had tasking to cover their zone, preventing any escape. Honor demanded vengeance. His people would extract it from the blood of these invaders.

Boris had a demolition pack for the communications building. One of the reinforcing family members had brought a homebrew signal jammer with him. Destroying the soldiers' communications capability could only help their rescue attempt. At worst, the destruction would at least improve the morale of Boris' force.

Once the two tanks (really APCs) exploded in flames, that jammer would be activated. Boris had three packets of explosives set for remote detonation, two with thermite packs attached to their bases. The blast and thermite packs were more than able to disable the APCs. Proper placement of the final packet would neutralize the communications building.

The mortar operators with his group were setting up to target the APCs and communications building. The mortarmen opposite were targeting the barracks. Each of the mortar teams had one of Boris's ex-mercenaries in the group manning the weapons. All companies had four or more ex-mercs for a small command group.

The groups deployed on every side of the base, enveloping it. The pack formed an assault group. Composed solely of Weres, including one other Werebear whose sister was among the murdered, moved forward. Flitting through the night, they would form the sharp spear tip of the assault. Most of them paused as soon as they were out of the sight of the human militia following them. Dumping their clothes, they changed to a deadlier form than their human one, then resumed their advance.

The power of the changelings would ignite, the animal cravings let loose.

The last company acted as a rearguard, following closely behind the Weres. Serving as both protection against any flanking attacks and insurance that no one escaped the deadly movement of rapid attackers, this force was the final barrier, the closing trap.

Boris crept forward looking for a gap or opening where he could get past the sentries. Neither of the APCs was manned. A group of sentries on the west side had closed up, leaving a gap in surveillance. Skulking in the shadows, he slipped through an opening as the guard meant to be watching this sector turned nervously. Perhaps the untrained fool needed to assure himself that others were there. Boris almost snorted. These were either green troops or something else masquerading as soldiers.

He carefully placed the thermite and demolition block combos under the turrets of the unmanned APCs. It felt a waste, but if the defenders manned them his attacking force would be in trouble. He looked at the communications building and placed the demolitions block on the side with the satellite dish and antenna farm. Only a little luck and all threat of enemy reinforcements would be negated. Boris was relieved by that. Relying on a homebrew jammer had made him nervous.

Quickly moving to the prison block on the southern edge of camp, Boris kept to the shadows and avoided the single internal patrol. By the gods, these were more like the SS guards he had fought in the Second World War than real soldiers. They had a veneer of training. Underneath, they had the discipline of thugs in uniform. He approached the prison block from the front and cursed. It was well lit all around sides, with a full squad guarding the door. It was possible they were some kind of political fanatics, and if so, he had to get into the building and protect the prisoners.

He weighed his choices. Option one was to detonate the demolitions charges and go Pricolici. But then he'd have to worry about the prisoners seeing him. The pack would have to deal with that later if they survived. Not a good choice. He quickly went through the other options but was stymied with the alertness of the guards. Weighing all the options, it seemed clear that several bursts from his weapon followed by a bayonet charge after he detonated the demolition combo was the best strategy.

Boris quietly connected the bayonet to his rifle. He lifted his head, silently watching for any alert and then nodded as much to himself as to any of his group who might be watching him.

It was time.

He pressed the button and detonated the charges. His face displayed a grim smile as he fired three quick bursts into the shocked and confused squad. Most of them died in the initial fire. He shook his head at their apparent lack of training.

He charged as he heard the whistle of incoming mortars. Shock was clear in the expressions of the two soldiers that survived his initial fire. He fired a burst into one of them as the man raised his rifle. The other's surprise lasted long enough for Boris's bayonet to slice into his throat and through his spine. Blood flew, cascading into the dirt.

Pulling the bayonet out Boris moved to the door and kicked it hard. The door slammed open. Boris found bedlam inside when he heard one of the men in the block shouting. "Get to the prisoners. We will use them as hostages. They want to save them. We can force them to negotiate!"

These *beschestiye* wouldn't get the chance.

Boris ran forward, remembering the layout of the base prison from a long-ago exploration after it was decommissioned. The next instant he caught up with the rear group. He noticed in passing that one of them had epaulets on the shoulders.

Boris fired a quick burst into the group, hoping he had missed the officer since they needed him for information. Now within fist range, his rifle dropped onto the floor. In a flurry of kicks, blocks and punches he knocked the remaining two unconscious.

Untouched except a nasty knife gash from the officer before the man fell to his assault. Boris drew a deep breath. The man showed the skill of serious training and was probably former military. The other was about as skilled as your average street thug.

He looked at the shoulder patch on the uniform of the closest body. A red field with a white tri-bar cross on it. The initials N.V.G. under the cross. Definitely not regular army.

Something close to pity flowed into Boris as he realized how lopsided the battle raging outside was. Street thugs against people trained over many years as a competent militia. His people would take casualties, but if they didn't surrender VERY quickly, the NVG contingent would be obliterated.

He quickly found the keys to the prisoner section in the officer's pockets and went to those rooms. Fifty people crowded in a space that was meant to hold twenty. Many of them had been beaten. Alecta recognized him and weakly shouted, "Boris." He nodded his head in recognition and acknowledgment and gave out orders to those inside as he yanked open the doors. The locks screeched as his enormous strength wrenched them open.

Within five minutes, those ablest had taken up weapons, looted from the five guards inside the building and supplemented with those of the dead squad members that Boris had mowed down in his assault.

As the former prisoners organized their defenses and armed twenty-five men, Boris kept a wary eye on the perimeter. He threw a grenade into a small group of attackers as they charged the containment area door, timing the throw to the momentary check that happened as they came upon the slaughtered guards and newly-freed prisoners.

With that effort, he was confident the twenty-five defenders could hold without him.

He ran fast and low out to the base. It was mayhem. More than half the NVG were down. There were the visible signs that the pack had taken out more 'strategic' targets. Anyone with the rank of corporal or higher seemed to have had his throat ripped out. Groups of the thugs were either throwing down their arms or throwing away their lives.

Twice as he cleared a path to Paul's group, he encountered an NVG group showing suicidal defiance. Twice he attacked them from behind, speeding them on their journey to hell. Suddenly he felt a sharp burn across his back and collapsed. As he slipped into unconsciousness, he cursed his own stupidity. He'd gotten into the middle of everything with no-one to cover his back. Before the darkness took him, knowledge of his people's victory warmed him

---

He awoke to hear a male voice tinged with irony saying, "Boss, we had it handled. You should have stayed with the prisoners, protecting them. We might have taken a few more casualties, but between you and the pack, they were broken. All we had left was cleanup. No need for you to take four in your back. If you'd at least wear your body armor, I wouldn't be saying this. When we finally broke through, the others saw about twenty wolves guarding your body. I think the fact you are different is not hidden anymore." Paul looked down at his friend, "You're gonna have an interesting meeting with the people. I doubt any one of them will stay away now. Gonna have to explain something boss. Well, two somethings. The wolves and how the hell you recovered so fast."

Boris shrugged, "Most of the families already know Paul. The elders and others who served with me at least."

He felt a twinge in his back as he tried moving his shoulders around.

Paul glared at him "Oh, now you tell me. You made me feel like what I knew was so secret I could be shot if I told anyone. Makes me seem like a bit of a fool."

Boris eyed him, "With your mouth and how you run it. If I hadn't told you, you would have mouthed off on a mission. Mouthing off would have gotten you killed."

Paul shrugged, neither admitting nor denying the accusation. He tended to be a smart ass, so denying that it might have slipped out was stupid.

"Who's in charge Paul? You should be with your wife. It's not likely I'll be lynched. I'll talk to them and get everything organized."

"That hunter, Danislav. He is tough enough and rowdy enough that no one will challenge him right now. A couple of the veterans are helping to organize and control. We have the injured heading to town in some of the trucks with the mercs who had medic training. We have thirty-one militia dead, and two wolves down."

"Go. Be with your wife. I'll sort out what needs sorting and trust the family elders to keep a lid on things for the time being in town."

Paul left, concern still clouding his face. His desire to be with his wife and assure himself of her safety was apparent, though. Boris was satisfied with that. He led a vicarious life through the families of those closest to him.

Boris stretched and looked around the room. The bullet that had hit him had missed everything vital. It also seemed to him that the treatments from Bethany Anne's machine had accelerated his healing capabilities. He rose and rummaged around the room he had recovered in. He found a shirt that would fit him. It was lightweight for a human, considering the weather. He would be fine.

When he headed outside, he found it was early afternoon. Boris could see from the flow of people where those who were giving orders were gathered, outside the wrecked communications building. That made sense. It was somewhat central to the camp. He sighed. He needed to find out how many were critically injured and should probably call Bethany Anne to see if there was anything she could offer in help.

First things first. Find out the numbers.

He approached Danislav, who grinned and said, "Ahh, our glorious leader graces us with his presence. Only you could lead such a successful action and get shot by the last enemy with any fight left."

Boris shrugged. "What is the situation on casualties, Danislav? Number of dead, critically injured, and severely injured, please."

"Thirty-three dead. Twelve critical, en route to the hospital in town. We may well lose four of them yet. But the last I heard they were stable. Over fifty with serious, but not life-threatening injuries. Of the assault force, we have three hundred and fifty capable of fighting, although many of them need rest. Over one hundred and twenty dead on the other side. Twenty captured, including a 'Major,' a commissar and two other officers."

"Be careful of the one I knocked out in the prison. He has serious military training." Boris rubbed his side remembering the cut he'd taken. There was no mark of it, but the memory carried an ache.

"Already noticed blood on his knife. He's got a rotation of two pack members watching him at all times."

"Have you got all this in hand? I need to go talk to someone who might be able to send aid."

Danislav smiled and nodded. "No worries. When do you want to schedule the town meeting you called?"

"I don't know yet. Part of that depends on answers from the call I will make. What do you think our people will decide?"

"I think you have a split. Probably two-thirds will go if you have somewhere safe for them to head. At least a quarter, more likely a third, want to take the fight to the bastards. In the pack, it's probably the reverse, and we have more packmates on their way here. If you can hold off until tomorrow, you'll have most of the Weres in Siberia in attendance. Joshua is bringing the tundra pack down by buses to the border of the province, then traveling the rest of the way in as wolves. With the stashes you made us maintain, we have enough to clothe everyone coming in that way. We have people arriving by plane and vehicle. Vassily is also on his way from Western Russia, by himself."

Boris spat on the ground at Vassily's name. "Put him in a room with some vegetables and water. He's the only person I can think of who might have revealed to the government I might be dead. I don't need a Were with links to the politicians spying on us." Danislav only nodded. Personally, he didn't believe Vassily was stupid enough to talk to his contacts about Boris unless he'd seen his body and checked that there was no pulse.

"While you were out, I took the liberty of talking to the Major and his commissar, separately. They are both convinced the army will drop in on us like a ton of bricks when they find out. Their formation is called the *Nashi vooruzhennye gruppy*. Basically, an armed wing of fanatics from the President's Nashi political movement. Both his captains are ex-military. One of them needed no threats to talk, though. The one who was outside trying to organize the defense."

"And what did he have to say? Stop playing games. I need to know this." Boris said impatiently.

"He said he thinks, especially if they find out about the shootings in town, that the military is more likely to move in to defend the town or stay in their barracks. Even if the President gave a direct order, no sane officer would follow it. It is too close to the genocide provisions in the Laws of War. He also explicitly states he protested the Major and Commissar's order. He asked if we have an exit plan. Or any method to smuggle him out of Russia. Even with a price tag of explaining to other governments the truth of events. He did, however, state that he refused to be quoted for the news. He seems to be genuinely ashamed of what has happened."

Boris nodded, storing that information in his mind. Bethany Anne may be glad for the info. The entire incident and the captured officers could well give her leverage over the Russian government. Or she might just kill them. Either way, he was happy to hand that decision off to her.

Boris pulled out the device he'd been given by Frank. He stepped away from the command group and walked towards the burned-out carcasses of the two APCs. The area was reasonably clear with no real traffic, so he turned on the mobile-like device and punched in the number

Frank had provided. He'd been assured it would work nearly anywhere and was secure.

"Carol speaking. How may I help you?" asked a female voice over the line.

"This is Boris. I was wondering if I could speak to either Frank or Nathan."

There was a pause. "If you can wait for a couple of moments, Bethany Anne wants a conversation with you." A malicious smile was expressed by the speaker through tone alone.

Boris sighed. It seemed that even her assistant knew something he didn't. Evidently, he hadn't pissed her off that much. Thinking about what Michael had said about her tendency to violence, he sure as hell hoped that she was not that pissed off.

He waited, sweating at the thought of how angry Bethany Anne might be. Boris hadn't thought about that aspect before, even though Stephen had said that she knew what her oath committed her to. He was too used to being the sole person who his people had for protection to have even considered anyone else and their thoughts or sense of obligation.

An icy cold voice spoke across the line. "Boris. I saw much of your assault. Why are you calling? Do you have more information? Or have you decided you need help, now you have your fucking macho bullshit out of the way?"

"Czarina, I apologize for any accidental insult I may have given. I am used to being the senior protector of my people. I only realized as I was waiting now that there may have been aid you could have offered without compromising your relationship with Russia. However..." He briefed her on what was happening. Part of that briefing was a suggestion that she come to the town meeting so he could pronounce her a fitting Czarina to receive the oaths of allegiance. He reminded her that those vows were effectively life-long.

"But I'm not a queen or Czarina or whatever you are talking about," She replied, her voice not nearly as ice-cold as it had been when she first answered.

"You were the woman who Michael loved. That makes you as close to a Queen that the UnknownWorld has ever known. You have power, and such a title generally comes with power. Finally, my people have spent almost a century in the wilderness waiting for their prophesied Czar or Czarina. Would you deny them someone to take their oaths and loyalty?"

"What about the fact I'm a Vampire? Will that cause any serious problems?"

There was silence as the issue hung between them. Boris sighed, "No, Czarina. Many of them already know of the UnknownWorld. I was... inventive in my interpretation of the Strictures, though word never reached Michael and it never bothered Peter. I think David may have known. He once tried to dump a plane full of Nosferatu on the town, but I foiled the operation. He knew my human support had such knowledge after that. Peter already had that knowledge, so it wasn't a real problem. It was a mistake for them to have joint responsibility for Russia, but political and geographical boundaries were such that it was considered the best solution."

"At least two-thirds of the town and surrounding population knows about Weres. I doubt that finding out vampires are real will be a problem unless you make a frightening appearance. Besides, if you can send something to help heal the critically and seriously injured they won't care. At all. They will owe you."

There was silence on the other end of the line, and finally, Bethany Anne sighed, "So I suppose this makes you the prophet whose predictions become real. Get back to me with a time. For the doses I'm giving you, I want you to take them from the landing site."

Boris interrupted, "Here in town. As soon as possible. I assume the vehicle you send with them will be similar to those you will arrive in. It will create a stronger sense you were responsible. If you can go into orbit, you can drop from the sky as well."

The tapping came along the line, then Bethany Anne continued, "I suppose I should listen to the advice of the man on the ground. Anything else I should know?" Boris gave her a summation of the information Danislav had given him. She finished the call with "I have to go. People to kill, politicians to terrify. You know how it is."

Boris waved down a vehicle heading to town as it was leaving the base. He'd left Danislav and the group assisting with the organization while his injuries had required healing. They seemed to have everything under control, so he left them to finish after telling them to organize the meeting for the next afternoon.

By then all Weres in transit would have arrived. It amounted to less than a fifth of the Weres in Siberia, but if that many came from as far as the Tundra Pack, he'd have a good feel for the overall opinions of the majority. Besides, he would give either Peter or Nathan permission to travel through the entire region and supply them with the locations of most of the packs and lone wolves. Not that he knew any of the lone wolves well. Siberia was just too vast to keep under a heavy thumb. His style was more relaxed, requiring rare intervention unless someone fucked up.

It took Boris about a half an hour to get into town. When the vehicle stopped near the town square, he stepped off and headed straight to the center. Just as he approached the area, a black shape plummeted from the sky. As it visually resolved into one of the Pods, he moved back a little from where it was to land. Once it came to a halt, Boris stepped quickly to the vehicle.

The door slid open on his approach. With the doors open, he could see the seat inside had a white case with a red cross emblazoned across the front. Boris grabbed it, turned around and ran straight to the hospital, hoping the use and dosage of any medications would be evident to those inside.

He burst through the doors and went straight to the nurse's station. He placed the case on the counter and opened it. The aid had come in the form of one hundred and fifty syringes with what looked to be blood or some other red viscous liquid in them.

He grinned but turned in alarm when he heard a patient monitor shrilling. Reaching into the case, he quickly grabbed a syringe. Running to the room with the loud noise resounded out into the hall, he stripped the cover off the needle. Without hesitation, he stabbed the needle into the dying militia man's chest.

Following him into the room was the doctor who

glared as he pushed him aside, the needle Boris used still in the chest of the patient. Before the doctor could even start resuscitation, the alarms suddenly stilled.

The doctor turned frustration and stress evident on his face, "What did you give him, Boris? Adrenaline? We need to know! You may have saved him only to have him die of complications you fool!"

Boris shook his head, "Nyet, Andre. I was sent some experimental medications that stabilize and heal. My contact and friend sent enough for our people. She will be at the meeting if you want to ask her about the contents. I was assured it will not complicate other medications, beyond reducing the time they are present in the bloodstream," Boris responded, extrapolating from his condition.

The doctor wasn't satisfied, "And do you have numbers on that? This is an immense complication, you idiot!"

"Doctor, pretend that you are treating Danislav or me, and that is your answer. They have replicated the healing of people like us without other effects."

The doctor stared at him, then back to the improved patient and then shook his head. "But it is still experimental?"

Boris stood there, thinking of a response. "Nyet. It has been tested, but not registered. The group that makes it does not want to be swamped beyond their production capabilities at this point. Though they were happy to give me some, in this time of need. This information, and how effective the treatment is, will need to stay here."

The doctor continued grumping as the two of them walked to the nurses' station. When they reached it, the doctor planned out the distribution to critical cases. With triage managed, he organized the schedule for the most severe cases. He chewed on a pen thinking about next steps. Well, next steps provided that there were no adverse reactions to the unknown medicine.

Boris would never deliberately harm the people he protected.

CHAPTER SIX

<u>Moscow, Russia</u>

Janna was cursing herself for following procedure last week. She had been ordered to come in for a debrief through drops, and she never trusted shrinks. It added risks, increasing the chance of her cover being blown. She was there to pose as the girlfriend of other agents if they needed it, and for that, she needed to blend into the background.

Turning up at a location many suspected was military controlled did not help with that. After the debrief, Janna had been satisfied her countermeasures had lost any possible tail on her, at least.

Losing any possible tail as she traveled back to her operational zone had taken time. That lost time she sorely missed as she caught up on the information drops. Once she finally had time to read them, the NVG had moved. It was by chance she received the direction the enemy was moving towards.

It was pure chance she'd been out, hoping to find more information at drop points when she'd received a message from a particular email address. The one her unit commander told her would always mean to go dark.

After sending emails of her own, from a similar setup, to the men under her command, she moved. For her, going dark was a personal setup. She walked north for an hour before catching a train to the southern edge of Moscow. Towards a particular site, one she had set up for herself. Building the cache had begun shortly after her commissioning. Everything had been paid for in cash. There was no official link between her and the owner, a retired librarian from her days on the street. As the only male librarian who had been both unmarried and had not propositioned her in late puberty, she trusted him.

She suspected he had his own secrets, and the money she had provided for the use of his lock up shed ensured that he would not feel used. If her suspicions were right and he was gay, he wouldn't want any official attention. Times were dangerous for anyone on the edge of 'acceptable society.'

On the train trip south there was a response from one of her men. A grid reference and a town name. Romanovka. Beside it was a code that translated to 'movement of armed men in force.'

The easy solution crumbled on her. She couldn't just disappear now. Another problem was that some towns with a Romanovka name in Siberia, where the coordinates placed it, were quiet strongholds of the old White creed. Waiting for a return to the Tsars. Prime targets for the NVG.

As she traveled to her bolthole, she considered everything. Especially Nashi and NVG propaganda. The town could be White, or it could be populated by regular citizens trying to survive. At least the hard drive she had packed would have background data on any town in Russia. She could work from there.

When she finally approached the shed, it was no surprise that the neighborhood was quiet. Slushy snow was falling steadily. Once she arrived at the bolthole, she grabbed out a sealed packet and typed a code into the phone within it. In hours, most records of her Army service would be wiped. In days only traces of her existence would remain in the system. Her wake up code would transfer the worm to any backup that was restored and connected.

Having friends in low places could be an advantage. By sending programming work to another former street rat, she had gained someone willing to make such a tool for her. Someone with shared experiences, unwilling to share what she had provided. And knowing the consequences if they crossed paths with Janna and had betrayed her. She was glad she had a sled fitting for the front of the motorcycle she had stored there. It would still be useful in this weather, although she was not planning on moving until the next dawn.

She had a fitful night's sleep. Information only one other had. Even then, he might not be able to act on it. She must decide. Try to save Romanovka or disappear from Russia into a quiet retirement. She'd fired up her laptop and her external drive and found it was a suspected White stronghold. Even with Mercenaries known to be operating out of Romanovka, there was a low threat rating. From what had been pieced together by Central Intelligence they would support someone with real proof they were the returning Tsars, and of the Romanov Bloodline. Otherwise, they would stay out of any conflict, except for the mercs.

Even those soldiers of fortune came closer to 'acceptable' standards than most in their line of work. Hiring them had been considered by the government for various 'Grey' and 'Black' ops. How they were hired was the problem. A notation said they had agents in Vladivostok and Archangelsk and a short list of missions suspected of having their participation. The evidence was circumstantial, and at least two of the missions had overlapping operational dates and struck locations thousands of kilometers apart.

If the town weren't White, the NVG would massacre the people there, claiming it had been. Use it as an excuse to start pogroms and lynchings across Russia. She felt a burning anger at the plan behind such actions.

After the fitful night's sleep, she concluded she had to act. It wasn't nationalism, nor was it loyalty to the current regime. Somehow she felt a kinship towards the people of the town. They were people thrown into circumstances they did not desire.

If her actions could prevent young girls from having to grow up on the streets, or could prevent their deaths, she had to take it.

Her luck held, especially on the weather side of travel. The sun was shining through as she dragged her vehicle to the street. After checking she had everything she might need, including a small amount of gold bullion for bribes, she replaced the lock that had been on the outbuilding with a red one.

It was a lock that would tell the owner he had space to use or rent as he wished.

CHAPTER SEVEN

Romanovka Town Square

Boris stood in front of a crowded square full of people whose scents told him of anger, grief, resolve. As he suspected, the crowd was large and included everyone from the surrounding area that could make it. While he could speak loudly, he couldn't shout with enough volume to allow all to hear.

At least ten thousand people were in the square, nearby public buildings, and streets. Boris stepped up and checked the microphone was on before speaking.

He started with praising the courage of those who had taken part in the attack on the NVG. He continued, explaining the danger he felt the shift in policy represented, official or otherwise. Finally, he announced "I called you all here for a Meeting of Decision, as I promised your ancestors. I have found someone worthy of taking up the mantle of Czarina of our people. She is not Russian. But challenging times need a change in our perspective.

She was loved by the only person to defeat me in combat. Is considered his equal. Events have shown in her a capacity for both ruthlessness when necessary and yet compassion when possible."

He waited for what he was suggesting to register on the crowd. Watching the expressions and actions of influential individuals and the crowd.

As the implication resonated, confusion and excitement ebbed and flowed through the crowd. Although many knew Boris was different, few had seen his other form. One loudmouth near the front was disputing Boris' right to call such without a meeting of the town council, half of whom had been shot. The loudmouth was punched out by one of the pack.

"Halt!" He got the crowd to stop for a second and look to him. He took off his cap and tossed it behind him where Paul guarded his back. "I will put an end to any concerns on my authority!"

Boris looked and his eyes furrowed.

The sound of shredding cloth echoed across the town, amplified by the microphone. The crowd gasped as one. Comments flew to the back. Descriptions moved as fast as people, passing details of the transformation to any out of clear sight of the stage. In the background, Paul grabbed a bag and pulled clothes from it.

His bear form roared, "Silence!" in a voice that seemed to shake the ground and the surrounding buildings.

"I did not protect yourrr people so you could become a rrrabble. I protected you, your fatherrs and your fatherrs fatherrs in faith for the future Czarr or Czarrrina. I promised to search and have done so. Now, with our greatest need, I found such a one!" His voice was rough but clear. Werebear Pricolici, for whatever reason, had always had better control over their speech than werewolf Pricolici.

There were some isolated shrieks in the crowd at his brutal looking form. The family and friends of those timid ones shushed them. Some in the crowd showed fear, but many showed a mixture of awe and rapture bordering on worship.

Legend walked among them. Not the legends they had been raised on, but those whispered around fires on cold nights. That among them some people were also 'other', protecting them from the worst of the outside world. Standing before them was the proof of their legends. Their stories had come to life and were standing in front of them, speaking to them, leading them.

Boris changed back, the shreds of his former clothing dropping to the ground and accepted a pair of pants from Paul. He put them on with no show or haste. Glaring out at the crowd when dressed, he stated, "Many of you knew about me. I give you the decision meeting. Although the person I found is... different, as I am. She lives now and has no small resources. She offered to take you in and swore an oath to protect you when I gave her a personal promise of aid. Without my asking, she has already sent us aid."

He gestured at more than a hundred people. Those injured in the assault, now out of the hospital and healthy. "I now ask for you to hear her offer."

As if they had been watching and waiting for him to finish, five black pods dropped from the sky to the area behind the podium that had been kept clear. First out were John Grimes, Akio, and Erik, followed by Ashur jumping down then Bethany Anne. Following this group was two of the Queen's Elite. Nathan and Peter exited the last pod.

As they approached the stage, Boris turned to Danislav and said. "Tie that loudmouth up and dump him at the edge of town. We'll move him outside of our territory after we finish this. He has shown a level of stupidity we don't need." Danislav nodded, picked the man up, slung him over a shoulder, and then headed off to take care of Boris' request.

Bethany Anne looked at what Danislav was doing and raised an eyebrow to Boris. He shrugged at her and mumbled, "In any group, there is always ONE idiot." She nodded in wry acceptance. Boris continued, "Please, give your speech and then we will head off to a distance. They have a right under the protection agreement to discuss their opinions amongst themselves without the candidate or me present if the candidate is not a Romanov."

Bethany Anne thought on that and decided that it was a surprisingly wise provision. She smiled at him and waited for what would come next.

Boris, along with the town elders and troop commanders who stood on the stage, exited it to the left. Bethany Anne entered the newly vacated space from the right. John, Erik, and Aiko took places on the stage front while the two Elites took silent positions to the side, guarding the steps to the podium.

Bethany Anne smiled as she spoke into the microphone, "Hello, my name is Bethany Anne, and if you do not realize it, I'm a Kurtherian-changed human, like some of you. The difference? I have been changed by one group, and those changes make me what folklore has called a Vampire. Some of you have been altered by another group, and those changes turn you into a Wechselbalg, a changeling. In a few cases, like Boris, the changeling can take an additional form, called a Pricolici."

She stopped a moment to let the information sink in. "I don't give a flying fuck what group changed you, what your parents did or the color of your skin. We care about two things. First is protecting this Earth. Allowing people here their own choices for the future, even bad choices. Our other focus is taking the fight to the Kurtherians trying to subjugate other races in outer space."

She looked down at the microphone.

ADAM, can you and TOM jack me into the announcement system?

>>Yes, one second.<<

Bethany Anne smiled at the group.

>>Done.<<

Bethany Anne walked back and forth on the stage, the distance from the microphone not causing a problem. "It won't be easy, it won't always be fun, but it will be the future. We are going to space, we are taking the fight out there," she said, as she pointed to the sky, "and we need people. People who aren't afraid of the future, people who can bring skills, intelligence, and passion. People who understand family because my group is a family. One of my closest female friends is a Pricolici, a werewolf, another is a vampire, and the third is a human."

She looked at the assembled people standing a few feet from the podium, yet her words were heard through the speakers everywhere, "To me, we are all people. Not Americans, South Americans, Russians, or Chinese. For most people on this earth, it will be a challenge they cannot comprehend or accept. They can't handle the savage frontier of space, but for those who have tamed Siberia?" She smiled looking around at the hardy people in front of her, "I doubt outer space holds much of a challenge for you!"

The roar of the crowd confirmed their agreement. The gathered people knew their worth, their resilience, backbone, even stubbornness. They were the ones who beat the savage weather and knew how to stick together to make a future happen.

Bethany Anne's kind of people.

She walked to the other side of the stage, the Bitch's stepping out of her way, "Our challenge now is to keep you as protected as we can without causing a major event. Once you hit the border, well, Russia can kiss my ass. We will have containers to get you to our base in Australia and are building our first space station to provide you with temporary quarters."

She held her head up, throwing her arms wide pointing to the crowd, "It will be YOUR job to help design the next space station, your home. I would suggest learning well and learning quickly." She pulled her arms back down, "Pull your best people for each area and work with our teams to gain knowledge of what is available and possible. We have to use manufacturing and trading capabilities from Earth to build our space facilities, but we are learning quickly how to procure our own resources out there. Be assured, unlike this country, I want you to join my team! We need you to help protect

Earth, and we want you to be a part of the future, a new future!"

The clustered mass of people exploded into cheers and loud calls for action. The combined excitement of what they had just heard and the relief from the previous day's acute danger had left the crowd in a flammable state, and Bethany Anne's speech had provided the fire for the fuse. Small groups of people were talking excitedly, with expansive gestures and loud exclamations.

Bethany Anne let them vent. She waited in silence as the yelling died down, as the crowd's attention returned to her. She spoke calmly, with passion, "Know this from the bottom of your feet to the top of your Russian heads, while I don't want to start a war with Russia if they bring in too much, I'll bomb them to the fucking stone age! You have my promise. I don't forsake my own, ever." Her eyes flashed red at the end, bringing the fact home to everyone there that this was a Czarina that wouldn't leave them to freeze out in the tundra.

Standing for a moment in contemplation, looking over the crowd, Bethany Anne presented an impressive figure to people that hungered for a leader. She walked down from the stage, and her guards formed up around her and headed to an alleyway that Boris had kept empty for them. They continued over to a building that was being guarded by members of Boris's pack.

"I checked the building before the meeting and set guards on it once we knew it was clear. If you feel that your people need to check, please feel free to do so," Boris said, waving a hand in invitation.

Nathan snorted when John seemed about to pick up his

pace. "If Boris's pack can't be trusted to follow his orders I'll jump in front of a train, John. They have either accepted his authority or left. It's how we are." Turning to Boris, Nathan asked, "How long has it been since someone has challenged for leadership of the pack?"

Boris looked at him and grinned, responding, "About a hundred and seventy years. And that time I was the challenger." Nathan turned to John "Let me put it this way, John. He knows as many or more possible 'hazards' as you do. If I were a member of his pack, I wouldn't cross him. Hell, before I was a Pricolici I wouldn't have crossed his second if I could avoid it. That guy is strong. So how about we head in? Boris has sworn an oath to Bethany Anne. He won't break it."

John looked at Nathan, then glanced in apology at Boris. "It's just..." Boris smiled and continued "Professional paranoia, I know. I have done bodyguard work on occasion. When the pay was right."

Boris checked the group that was following Bethany Anne and nodded when he saw that all of them had followed. "Thank you for following the spirit, not just the letter, of my agreement. I assure you no harm will come to your craft." Bethany Anne just smiled and said. "No, it won't. If someone approaches them, the Pods will go up to two-hundred feet and hover there."

Boris nodded. He knew his people. Any such approach would be more a part of a passionate discussion rather than an intent to damage or steal.

While they waited, Bethany Anne picked his brains for whatever he knew about the UnknownWorld situation in Russia. Nathan nodded on specific details, and frowned on others, depending on whether the information matched or conflicted with what he already knew.

In just over an hour a runner from the crowd arrived. He knocked on the door and waited until John opened it. The messenger looked up at the tall man and explained, "We have reached a consensus. All agree that someone willing to be that open with her goals, and the challenges to achieving them, is worthy. However, there is disagreement with how best we might serve. A significant number wish to remain behind, to disperse and serve as your eyes and ears in Russia. If necessary to serve as your fist. Some feel we cannot leave. They wish to remain to crush the force that was used against us so that other groups not as fortunate in protectors and friends are not so ill-used."

Boris commented before Bethany Anne could respond, "This is not loyalty to the government but instead a statement of faithfulness to you and your goals. Some love the concept of Russia and the land we have cared about for centuries. But Russia under an iron fist is likely to look elsewhere. Find external causes to blame for internal problems Keeping a presence here will help to keep Russia from being crushed under the weight of the political agenda, stupidity, and greed. It will contribute influence over the troublemakers."

She looked at him, considering. "Are you volunteering to stay and lead them?" she asked. "If they swear an oath to me, they are welcome to come and damn the other consequences. But if some wish to stay I won't stop them if you honestly believe it will help and they are working under a leader they, and I, can both trust. Otherwise, the consequences can go fuck themselves. I couldn't care less."

Boris shrugged, "I swore to serve you as best I could here, on this world. If some of my people wish to stay and aid me in that, then I welcome their assistance. Especially if we can have additional medicine before the combat is joined this time." He said the last with a grin. Bethany Anne looked at him carefully and sensed the truth, or at least his belief in that reality, behind his words.

Bethany Anne paced, "Okay. I have two other conditions though. Everyone under sixteen is going. Anyone too old to assist you is going. Those are not negotiable. I won't leave people for the slaughter." She stopped to get a nod from Boris that he heard, "The second is that you are now responsible for Russia. If there is an UnknownWorld problem, find it and fix it. Ask for help if you even *might* need it."

Boris looked at her thoughtfully. It was evident to him she had a reason to trust him so much. Then he remembered the aura of fear that Michael had given off the night they fought. The other abilities Michael was rumored to have.

Boris nodded "I accept. I suspect if I did not, and Russia became a problem, you might resort to extreme measures to solve the problem. That might not be the best solution." He said it with a smile, but Aiko and the two Elites tensed. John waved them down. It wasn't disrespect, it was a statement that the best solution wasn't always a hammer - or a rain of Pucks.

She returned his smile and shook her head. "I doubt I'd do anything too extreme - at least across a large area. The government might lose a few obstreperous members, though."

Boris shook his head. "Unfortunately, here in Russia, that would only focus anger on the West. Perhaps with catastrophic results. The reflex reaction of most Russians would be to decide that the West was assassinating our leaders. Whoever took over would likely ride the emotional wave of anger to advance their control and agenda. If the new leaders tried to resist, popular pressure might force their hand."

Bethany Anne pointed to him and said, "See - I knew you were the right person to be in charge of this area."

Boris looked at her concern evident on his face and put up a hand, "As long as someone else looks after China. I want no responsibility for that ratfuck."

Captain Janna Dmitrievna was pissed off. Her mission for Russian military intelligence had started simple. Infiltrate Nashi, find out any armed or militant formations that might be recruiting. Report back. When her reports indicated that radical factions were developing in the Nashi, it earned her a promotion and orders to organize and lead a more comprehensive infiltration of those groups.

That was when she found out that military-grade equipment was being diverted to the factions and that they were training in company and battalion-sized operations.

Then Janna learned that a reinforced company was being sent on an 'internal removal' operation against a town known to be populated by White Russian descendants. It was the Nashi's political rhetoric that there were only Russians. No Reds, Whites, Greens or other factions. That for Russia to be healthy, unity was vital.

Nashi in and of itself wasn't an issue. It was the fanatics that joined this armed wing, the NVG, that was a concern. They were careful in their recruitment. It had taken three months to get a single person inside, out of the thirty people she had assigned to the operation. But something had leaked to destroy her information sources. She'd been told a week ago that the agents' covers were blown, that they were in the cold.

Within hours of Janna's finding out about the problem, the NVG were moving against a small town in Siberia. She'd had no contact with half her operatives since then, not even on tertiary channels. Her only hope was they had scattered to their safe sites. She set up a rallying point for the remaining operatives that retained contact with her since her prime moral duty was to them.

She also felt a responsibility to do what she could for the town under attack. They were Russians. They had been loyal. There was no reason to attack them because of their ancestry.

For three days she'd been traveling, knowing the NVG would beat her to the town. Bracing herself for a massacre. When she passed an abandoned militia base, it was apparent that combat had taken place there. She pulled off the road, got off her motorcycle and looked around. She recognized at least two destroyed APCs and a couple of wrecked military trucks. It looked like mortar fire damage.

Which side had mortars?

She needed to go into town and gather more intel. Getting back on her motorcycle, she rode forward into town. As she approached the edge of town, she was waved to halt by one of the local police.

Shit.

Everything was going wrong if police had sided with the NVG. She slowed down, thinking to turn her bike around and head back. Maybe try to infiltrate after it was dark. Perhaps go back to her team, see what plan they could pull together. As she slowed down, three men rose from concealment pointing their rifles at her.

Shit on a stick. An ambush for people coming into town. There was no way back.

One of them shouted, "Turn off your engine, get off your vehicle and keep your hands in sight." She quickly estimated the odds in her head and decided that her best option was to comply and attempt an escape later on. They were not likely to know she had been in intelligence since she carried nothing that was military. There was a better chance of escape than dodging bullets from three assault rifles. Following their instructions, she got off the bike and waited.

Deciding to be as non-threatening as possible, she started to shake slightly, as if in fear. One man slung his rifle and approached cautiously, keeping clear of the other's line of fire. He gave her a professional pat down, and she was glad that her sidearm was hidden in the bike saddlebags. That pistol would have given away her past to the degree that could only cause her more difficulties. Then she was handcuffed.

The man who had waved her down had been talking to someone on the radio, and a police car was quickly approaching from town. It looked like the NVG had lost whatever disagreement had occurred between them and the townspeople. That meant that the NVG had been staying at the old military base she had passed. It also suggested that the mortars had been used by the townspeople. Shit, again.

Talk about your intelligence fuckups.

What information she had accessed before being dumped in the cold had shown maybe forty or fifty active mercenaries living in the town, supplemented by an equivalent number of retired mercs. At least half the active ones were away on operations at any time. So seventy-five professionals, and maybe another hundred former conscripts of recent service had been her estimation. Not the battalion with indirect fire she estimated an assault on the base required to avoid massive casualties. From the looks of the base, the town possessed a well-armed, well-trained militia. One local military intelligence had not picked up.

The police car pulled up. Forcefully placed in the back with a uniformed police officer next to her. "Take her to Boris," was the only commentary as she was transferred to the car. She wondered who this Boris was. The Chief of Police was not named Boris. The only person of note in the town named Boris was a mercenary. Well, THE mercenary she supposed, although the file was confusing. It had a history going back to the fifties. The photo of him dated only three years past showed a man in his thirties. He had trained all the other mercenaries currently active originating from this region, but the file included no details on where he had received his training.

As the car drove off, she saw one of the four there take

her bike towards a nearby barn. She realized they were manning a subtle checkpoint.

At least her clothes and equipment wouldn't get wet.

There was a knock on the door. Boris looked towards Bethany Anne and spoke, "They would only interrupt now if they felt it was something I - I mean we - should look into." He turned to the runner. "Inform the meeting of the proposed Czarina's conditions. If they agree, get the elders to organize the volunteers. Make it clear I have final approval on any who volunteer, and they will have to be fit to serve. The Czarina would have my head if I accepted anyone who could not contribute with a good chance of survival." Bethany Anne nodded at his last comment. "Enter," he said more loudly, as the runner headed to the door.

A police officer, one of the retired mercenaries, entered the room. He said "We brought in a woman approaching the town. Considering the timing, I felt it was suspicious enough to bring her to you. No one else unexpected or from outside the locality has arrived today." He saluted.

"Let's see her. It's probably nothing, but the timing is odd. I can make sure she can't hurt you in any way," Bethany Anne said.

The woman entered the room. She was tall, about five feet eleven inches tall. With long blond hair and pale skin, her face was intense, with Tartar features, displaying an exotic beauty. Bethany Anne felt Boris tense beside her. She looked at him and saw his face, never usually tan, was whiter than usual. His expression wasn't giving anything away. In fact, he seemed to have frozen it into one of non-expression.

Boris, what is it? Do you know this woman? Bethany Anne spoke directly into his mind. She couldn't hear or feel anything from Boris. It was as if he'd locked down his thoughts and emotions.

Then she heard a soft whisper from his mind. *Still, like a calm pond.* Repeated continuously, a mantra of desperation.

Gott Verdamnt! Boris tell me what the problem is, or I will rip off your arm. I am not made of glass. I need to know the problem so we can solve it! She practically shouted in his head.

Boris glanced at her and sighed. Then, responding with his thoughts, *She could be the sister of the woman I loved a century ago. The one executed by the Reds. It took me by surprise is all. Especially since she even smells the same.*

Bethany Anne felt intrigued by this. Boris's devotion to his old lover's memory was apparent in the effort he had taken to keep his oath to her. His reluctance to explain was reasonable. He didn't want to poke Bethany Anne's recent wounds and was trying not to be overcome by his older ones.

Luckily, TOM had a handle on her grief, which Boris had no way of knowing. She had too much to do, although she still spent at least an hour a day alone in a pod dealing with all the unfiltered emotions of agony, frustration, and grief.

Forcing Boris to explain caused him to lose the grip he had held his emotions in. Standing motionless next to her, he was a roiling mess behind the stony facade. It even seemed to affect his etheric signature. *I've got this.*

Bethany Anne turned towards the woman and asked, "And you would be?"

Janna's mouth opened and then quickly shut before she could speak. A desire to answer with the truth filled her. Had they somehow injected her with some truth drug while she was on the way here?

Bethany Anne was intrigued. This woman was trying to resist her command, so this person was someone out of the ordinary. Possibly, she supposed, up to no good. Giving the strange woman the benefit of the doubt, her resistance suggested that she had no one here known or trusted. Even with that explanation, there was something weird about the resistance to Bethany Anne's mental pressure. Anti-interrogation training, maybe.

Bethany Anne sighed and issued the command harder, "Look, if you don't answer me, we are in for a very long afternoon. So you may as well answer. My name is Bethany Anne. Who are you and what is your *job*?" She supplied maybe fifty percent more force than she used for Silvens-Werner.

Without realizing she would speak, Janna answered, "Janna Dimitrievna. Captain, Russian Military Intelligence. At least until a week ago." Externally she kept her composure. Internally she was cursing up a storm.

What had she been dosed with? Fuck. She'd scored high in interrogation resistance, even when drugged. But whatever they were using was cutting right through it. Then she thought she saw a slight red glow from the interrogator's eyes and felt an involuntary shiver go through her spine.

"And what were you doing here?" Bethany Anne continued.

"I came to Romanovka to see if I could help the people against the Nashi *vooruzhennye gruppy*. They were the group I was investigating before my team and I were disavowed. The last piece of information I received from inside the group regarded this attack. And it may have cost as many as fifteen lives to get. I would not want those lives wasted!"

Bethany Anne's face softened. "Ah. So you aren't here to support the attack, and you have, effectively, been fired and left to survive or die on your own?"

"Yes," Janna replied through a grimace, "though I hope to link up with some of my team. I doubt any of us would make it through a regular border crossing, though. I'm sure our faces are now flagged."

Boris finally spoke. "My name is Boris. I wonder, are you a patriot, Janna?"

She looked at the man, trying to match the face in front of her to the photo from the folder, "Explain. That's a question with many meanings."

Boris glanced at Bethany Anne with a twinkle in his eyes, "Are you loyal to the people of Russia, or the government?"

Janna glanced between the two and settled back to Boris, "People are more important than politics."

Bethany Anne laughed, "A humanist who worked in intelligence. I would have sworn we would find an alien before we found a moral intelligence agent."

Bethany Anne asked the Russian intelligence officer, "What if I told you we are facing a bigger problem for the entire human race? That if you were willing, you could help your country and the people of Russia by helping the world? I do not expect you to believe my word without proof. I'll show you."

At that point, Janna's eyes opened, and she cursed herself again. Damn, she had seen this woman before. Her brain must be sludge for her to have taken so long to put two and two together. This was the CEO of the company sending people into space.

CHAPTER EIGHT

Romanovka, Chelyabinsk Oblast, Siberia, Russia

Boris was tired. Sleep wasn't a likely option either. He had five thousand volunteers for the action group. He'd picked a hundred from them quickly. They had either served with him or had exceptional service records for their military service. That filled out the officers. He was planning on spreading both officers and operatives in a wide dispersal, using pods if necessary to travel between locations. Only five hundred agents per area, but just seven proposed areas of operation. It wasn't like they were expecting to set up bases or open resistance. They were planning to gather intelligence and fight limited actions against the NVG.

Satellites would find it hard to impossible to get an exact count on the refugee column. Janna had been vetted by Bethany Anne, and she agreed to help, her current military knowledge was put to use in planning a route to the Mongolian border that kept to the highway as long as possible while avoiding all population centers.

His people would travel slowly. The modified course added several days, but within three weeks they would be safe. The first group had gone ahead with half the Tundra pack and large strings of horses for the cross-country section. Half the refugee column would be required to walk out after they were forced to leave the highways. Only so many vehicles were available with off-road capabilities. That included the fifty military trucks they had scrounged and those captured from the NVG.

The tundra pack had, to a wolf, decided to join the Guardians. This would expand the Guardians by two hundred and fifty wolves. Two dozen 'lones' that they tolerated in their territory had also joined. Some Wechselbalg wolves did not appreciate company, similar to the majority of bears. The lure of adventure was attractive enough to overcome the aversion.

He had the officers and those who had volunteered to stay behind organizing the packing of supplies. Each person could take what they could carry on their back in personal possessions. Any off-road vehicle that had cargo-only space was being loaded to capacity with supplies.

Danislav knocked then entered the room. He spoke abruptly, "Boris, at least half the wolves are leaving for the Guardians. Might be more once word reaches those missed the meeting."

Boris shrugged and said, "Their choice. If I was a century younger and wasn't the best person to keep a lid on Russia, I might choose that too."

Danislav snorted at the idiocy of the comment, "No, you wouldn't. Have you got the officer list for the Czarina? She wants to get an early start on making sure your choices are right tomorrow, so she isn't tied up here for too long."

Boris passed the folder over. It listed each person's proposed position and relevant experience.

"Oh and Boris, I'd take Vassily over to her first. I wouldn't keep him trapped under guard for too much time. He has a temper. But with his contacts, he could be useful if he can be trusted."

Boris only grunted. He didn't trust Vassily at the moment, but if he had proof that someone else had caused this mess Danislav was right. Boris looked at the clock. Time to sleep a little before he needed talk to Vassily, though.

Janna was surprised that she had been called to this early meeting with Boris and Bethany Anne.

Yesterday Bethany Anne had done as promised. Janna blushed at the memory. When the pod had gone straight up, she'd grabbed Bethany Anne's leg. The response had been "You are cute. If I were a man, I'd be flattered, but I don't swing that way so *remove your fucking hand.*"

At least she had remained relatively calm when Bethany Anne had shown her true nature. She was unsure of how good her control had been, but Bethany Anne assured her that there had been many reactions that were far more extreme. Her trying to open a Pod door into vacuum didn't make her feel that her response had been rational at that moment.

Janna shook her head. She now knew more than Boris

about what was happening, including a lot about him. Although she was unsure regarding his capability to think clearly around her. With what she'd been told in private, her new boss insisted that a woman was needed on his command team who didn't look at him with awe. The implication was that Janna would be Boris's aide de camp.

Boris had accepted that, though he had given Bethany Anne a strange glare. Then he'd put Janna to work organizing and planning. It had been midnight before she'd gotten to bed. She felt she had barely slept when a polite woman woke her - at five AM.

When she walked into the meeting area, Boris and Bethany Anne were seated at a table with an empty chair to one side. There was a hot breakfast laid out buffet fashion. She noticed that Boris had a massive pile of food on his plate which he was attacking with a vengeance. When he looked up, he waved to the chair next to Bethany Anne.

"Come, sit, eat. We are about to interview a person who might either be very useful or has condemned himself to death for his actions. First, you need breakfast."

He was glad Bethany Anne, with her ability to either sense or force truth, hadn't left yet. He wasn't entirely sure he trusted his own opinion on Vassily. It would be good to have a second opinion on those he was making officers.

Bethany Anne looked at him, shaking her head. She had finally met someone who could easily eat more than Peter. What Janna didn't know was that this was Boris's third plate. Bethany Anne hated to think how he'd survive without food.

He has a draw on the Etheric. The dataset we have

from his time in the pod shows he would suffer no ill effects. He may just enjoy eating.

Thanks, TOM. I didn't think that one through did I?

You have a lot on your mind. I only informed you, so there was one less thing for you to worry about.

As Boris finished his meal, there was a knock on the door, and Vassily was led in. He blinked when he saw Bethany Anne and was obviously far more nervous.

Boris started the discussion, "So Vassily. You thought I was gone and sought to butter your bread by pointing out the history of this town to your 'friends' in the government."

Vassily looked even more nervous now. "No Boris. I swear. I came because I discovered who told them. I knew as soon as your last contract sponsor refused to provide a photo of your body you weren't dead. Then I heard one of my government informants let slip about the force coming here. Saying the mercenary in residence was dead according to Phillip Simmons. He was on the list of contacts that use that method of contacting me. So it all added up in my mind."

Vassily continued, "I came as soon as I found out. At worst you weren't back yet, and I'd help Danislav harass this NVG. At best you were, and I could give you the information and help as I could. I wasn't trying to cross you. I didn't think the mission you were contracted on was the big screw! I researched the mission as I usually do, no red flags came up. As far as I could tell it was a standard request. For you at least."

Boris looked at Bethany. She nodded at him.

Boris turned and tried to keep his annoyance off his

face. "Very well, I'll grant that none of the consequences were deliberate on your part." Vassily relaxed at that. "Still, do you acknowledge a debt? And are you willing to work it off?"

Vassily looked up "I will. But what will make you believe that I'm telling the truth?"

Bethany Anne snapped to capture his attention, then her eyes glowed red in the dim office light, "I'm the reason he will believe you." Vassily's heart beat harder, his forehead broke out in sweat and nearly fainted. He hadn't realized she was a vampire.

He got his tongue back under control, "Thhhen you kn-kn-know I'm sincere?"

Bethany Anne reverted to her regular human appearance. "Yes. You have been honest and sincere." She turned to Boris and said "You can trust him. I'll send you the modified cell phones before the storm hits."

She rose from her chair and left the room.

Vassily had left yesterday to pump his sources for more information on the NVG. The custom phones had arrived before Vassily had left. TOM and ADAM had assured Boris that they were secure. ADAM also mentioned he was setting up secure communications, and he would send details to each team leader. Janna had explained ADAM to Boris. She was confident ADAM could keep the merely curious and the hackers out. Everyone who stayed would get new identities and papers courtesy of ADAM, with Frank's help.

The phones were protected from tampering and were secured by voice recognition when using the Etheric connections.

None of Boris' officers were to take that equipment into operations. ADAM had set up a website secured by himself for other means of communication. Each team would have their own section, each team member a login. ADAM promised to give Boris and Janna a synopsis each day.

Boris had spent hours reviewing lists of volunteers. First, he'd narrowed it by removing at least one parent from each family with children under sixteen. Then he took out those few with university educations. Then, the eldest was removed, making an occasional exception for those who were skilled hunters, trackers, or listeners. That brought the numbers of people staying down from over five thousand to around three thousand, seven hundred and fifty.

He decided that was enough reduction. They were likely to take casualties when they finally faced the NVG to dismantle it.

He was putting off the next task. Paul wanted to talk to him. He suspected the reason, and it was causing him worry. He had hoped Paul would go with the group headed into space. Boris had taken him into enough hairy situations over the years, but Paul had come through those successfully. Selfishly, Boris just wanted the man who was probably his closest human friend to be safe.

Boris had spoken to his friend earlier, and it was only two seconds before Paul had insisted that he was too skilled and experienced to waste in space. Even worse, he was probably right. But Alecta was not happy with being separated from her husband. Although she would be comparatively useless to the group that was staying behind.

She was one of the worst shots Boris knew. She still flinched while pulling the trigger. With a Master's degree in metallurgy and a Bachelor's degree in geology and mining, space-borne operations needed her. Five years of industry experience added to that. Even after time out of the industry since returning home to settle with Paul and have a family. The boys were twelve and fifteen, so at least one of their parents had to go with them.

There was a knock on the door. It was Paul, as Boris expected. "Come."

Paul entered the room looking a bit sheepish. "Boss, can you talk to Alecta? She's saying she'll hand over guardianship of the kids to her aunt to make sure she's eligible to stay. I told her it wouldn't fly, but she's convinced that it will. She claims I'd talked to you before to make sure she would be leaving. I've asked her when I could have, but you know how she can be when she gets a bee in her bonnet. I pointed out that in ten years she still hadn't learned to not flinch when she pulled the trigger, but…"

Boris sighed. He did not need this, but Paul was an old friend. To his surprise, Janna spoke up in the sudden silence, "Paul, I placed you in our small command group. That is you, Boris and myself. You are third in command. But Alecta has no military experience, nor a reputation as a hunter, tracker or a decent shot. She'd be useless to the group compared to what she could contribute to the space-borne group."

She paused, then shrugged, and said. "I think this is where we pass it up the chain Boris. I'll call Cheryl Lynn. Explain, and see if we can expedite her transport to the design group. That way she won't play games. Hopefully, whatever task they give her will keep her too busy to have other worries."

Boris turned to her and grinned, his relief palpable, "And that is how a good aide works out the little things. Paul, you could learn from her. We'll get back to you as soon as it's arranged."

Hopefully, the NVG couldn't organize anything else before they were ready to move. They were now only waiting for a storm to cover the area. When that happened, they could travel without any additional assistance. The cloud cover would make everything easier.

Unfortunately, the weather had not co-operated. It had taken another five days before they had enough clouds overhead to cover their split and scatter movements. During that time the NVG had started a pair of reinforced companies moving towards the town. The same night Boris found out about the force approaching he had moved his people into ambush locations.

The experienced fighters were all in a position to perform attritional 'shoot and run' encounters. Half would scatter to their targeted areas of responsibility after each bushwhacking. The rest would fall back to the main force. The NVG was moving by back roads, avoiding highways. After three sprung traps, Boris expected them to switch to an alternate route. He had forces of approximately twelve hundred and fifty set along each of the probable routes into town. The plan was to wipe the NVG out to the last man.

They had time. ADAM predicted that the cloud cover would last at least ten days. The NVG planned to arrive in three. Boris expected them in about five.

Once they knew the attack route from their interception of communications and scouts verification, Boris would consolidate his forces. Four hundred or so troops against his nearly three thousand. He doubted his casualties would be even between 50-100. Particularly with the extra doses Bethany Anne had provided for his medics, nurses, and doctors. The mercs had unboxed and prepared their portable anti-armor weapons, and there were enough to take out any APCs.

Each officer had access to an account provided jointly by himself and Bethany Anne. These would provide funds for them to disburse to the troops so that working would not be necessary, although many of them would as part of their covers.

Boris had allowed for four weeks of travel for the refugee column to get to safety. It was, he hoped, a generous schedule. The extra time allowed Bethany Anne to provide a piece of equipment that Janna had requested. A camouflaged mobile command base that would permit them to travel quickly and discreetly between areas of operation. What Team BMW had produced looked like a rusting shipping container. It was modified to fly like the pods and had enough internal power to run communications and essential computer support. A small kitchen, first aid equipment, and beds were also included.

It also included, somewhat to Boris's distress, three motorcycles for local transport. Boris hated riding the damn things but agreed they made sense. Motorcycles could go places that cars couldn't, so they could hide the shipping crate in the wilderness most of the time, safe from prying eyes.

The countdown to Retaliation had begun.

FINIS

AUTHOR'S NOTES – PAUL C MIDDLETON

JULY 14, 2016

This journey started in late February. The 24th I think. I had just contacted Michael after reading book 4 of The Kutherian Gambit.

I was so disappointed that he'd taken the easy way out and gone with a *Katana* of all things as her sword.

I HATE how Katanas have taken over as sword of note in fiction. I call it the 'Highlander effect'. There is a two thousand word rant on my blog explaining.

So I joined facebook to contact him (Yes I was one of the very few people in my age group without an account.) And to bitch about his choice of sword. We talked a bit further and I mentioned I was trying to write a book. So he asked me if I wanted to join the 20books group. I was either member five or six (there are now over 300 I think.)

Then I kept coming up with a Russian Werebear character. One that in no way fit for my story. I named him Boris and eventually (three or four books of Michael's later) saw that he was a good fit for Michael's universe. So I wrote up a three thousand word Character concept/history and sent it to him.

That is where this book and the ones to follow came from.

That's not to say that there haven't been a few bumps along the way. But I think Both Michael and I have learnt that the best communication involves at least voice chat. It is so much easier to make sure there is no misinterpretation if you speak rather than type (Little advice for ANYONE who wants to write a collaboration! Speak! Typing only conveys so much!)

I've learnt a lot writing in someone else's universe. And I have nothing but Thanks to Michael for giving me this opportunity. I hope you all enjoyed it. Now … if I can only convince him to come up with a character in MY universe some time

Maybe.

I also have to thank My Beta Team for this project. Bree Buras, Dorene Johnson, Diane Velasquez and Kat Lind.

A thanks to both Nikolaus Beattie and Jeff Morris for helping me work out military details I was unsure of. (One is Australian Army, One US Army. Had some differing opinions, but between them they gave me the info for realism I needed to get stuff right for the book.)

You can reach me at any of these places. I do my best to respond quickly but I do live in Australia – Time zone issues and all that.

Blog: https://betrayedbyfaith.wordpress.com/

My Series Facebook: https://www.facebook.com/Betrayed-by-Faith-1110766018944080/

My Author Facebook: https://www.facebook.com/PaulCMiddleton/

My mailing list: http://eepurl.com/bZxFvD

My Amazon Author Page: http://www.amazon.com/Paul-C.-Middleton/e/B01FM3QX6E/ref=dp_byline_cont_ebooks_1

The Paladin book page: My Book

I love this. I get to be the last person to write my author notes, so I get a peek into what Paul wrote and then say whatever the hell I want.

Which, should probably be nice as I imagine Paul will get to switch places with me for book 2 ... *damn*!

Have you ever received a message that starts with "I like this...but!" Yes, the exclamation point is there on purpose. Paul's NO KATANA email should go down in history as some sort of Martin Luther'esque comment nailed to the door of Author's homes everywhere.

He admitted to me that out of about ten authors he has taken to task over using katanas, I was the only author who replied and struck up a conversation. I'm still trying to figure out how smart that was. Paul can get pretty excited when talking swords, something I'm not exactly an expert with. The only way I was able to 'win' the argument was showing how Bethany Anne did have the grip and strength to wield a katana with one hand effectively.

One point for super-strong modified humans!

Even then, Paul will not concede the point whatsoever. So, somewhere he has the original document about swords, you should hit him up and ask him. Or heck, he might have it on his blog.

It is a weird experience to have your world written in, and characters you know as friends to be written by someone else. My job, once we hashed out the general storyline and agreed on what could and couldn't happen based on future events, was to come back after Paul wrote most of the book. Then, I would either add to sections where he pointed something out (I need you to add fight scene here, or write Bethany Anne's speech here) or to modify special characters actions and speech to confirm they would sound the same as I would write them (Bethany Anne, etc.).

By the end of the book, Paul had his groove on pretty well.

I was adding to this book and doing my pass on the plane coming to Las Vegas and finished while here. When I got to the last sentence, I was wondering where the hell the rest was??? Damn! I was enjoying it and didn't want it to stop.

So, if that is how I, the series creator feels, I certainly hope you enjoyed The Boris Chronicles and look forward to the next in the series.

Now, if you Pitchfork and Matches fans would just light a fire under his ass, it would be much appreciated.

Forever grateful for readers and fans, beta-readers and our editor (see names up front...No, you really want to - trust me),

Michael Anderle

Betrayed by Faith

- Book 1 – Paladin
- Book 2 - A-Viking
- Book 3 – Myrmidon (3rd Quarter 2017)

The Boris Chronicles (Kurtherian Universe, With Michael Anderle)

- Book 1 – Evacuation
- Book 2 - Retaliation
- Book 3 - Revelations
- Book 4 – Title pending (2nd Quarter 2017)

Short Story Contributions to Anthologies

- Inanna's Circle Game, Volume 4 (edited by Kat Lind)
- The Expanding Universe, Volume 1 (edited by Craig Martelle)

These can be found and will be published on Paul C Middleton's Author page.

WANT MORE PAUL C MIDDLETON?

Join Paul's Email List here: http://eepurl.com/bZxFvD

Join Paul's Facebook Group Here: https://www.
facebook.com/Betrayed-by-Faith-1110766018944080/